I0518228

LAYOVER

LaMonte M. Fowler

VICENDIA MEDIA

CHICAGO

This is a work of fiction. Names, characters, businesses, places, events and incidents are either the products of the author's imagination or used in a fictitious manner. Any resemblance to actual persons, living or dead, or actual events is purely coincidental.

Cover Illustration Copyright © 2017 "L.I.F.E." by Karim Fakhoury

Copyright © 2017 LaMonte M. Fowler

First Edition (Updated)

All rights reserved.

ISBN: 0984874194

ISBN13: 978-0984874194

For Mom.

Thanks for the Science Fiction Book Club membership when I was ten. Without it, these words might never have come to pass.

ACKNOWLEDGMENTS

Before you dive into this story I want to call to your attention some of the people who made this story possible.

Many thanks to my dear friend Alexander B. Rossino, PhD. for his excellent editing and commentary on the story. Deep gratitude to my son Thomas Fowler for his beta reading and notes. His instincts about characters and tone always surprise me.

I want to also thank Canadian artist Karim Fakhoury for licensing his digital painting "L.I.F.E." to me for use as the cover of the ebook. The image was a fan favorite and I think it provides a deeply meditative enticement to explore this story. You can see more of Karim's work at http://karimfakhoury.com/.

And finally, I'd like to thank all the people who helped me select the cover art for this short story. As promised, here are the names of each person who took the time to review the options and express a preference: Amanda Fisher-Alberson, Chris Hubbard, Sandra Nicholas, Karrie Sedlmeyer, Perry A. Reynolds, Laura Goodwin Kabel, Jennifer Zapf, Kathy O'Brien Moore, Donna Waters

Peebles, JeanMarie Balkovec Kleppick, John Walker, JL
Schuyler, Allan Marsh, Keith Jenkins, Rebecca Wilson
Thomas, Patricia Terhune Anfora, Amy Alberda-Acosta,
Fiona Rankin, Kathy Bolain, Elizabeth Hafstad Behrendt,
Jan Stearns, Rhonda F. Paulson, Randall Patrick
McMurphy, Nicolette van Erp, Sandy Lear, Connie Jean
Monroe, Jodi Obeid, Michele Duggan, Cheri Lovell,
Susanne Smith, Lisa Hoyer, Karen Whinihan Nouwens,
Mariah Bishop Hudson, Linda McLaren, Cheryl Willetts,
Vivian Bofetta, Jean McCracken, Jamie Harrison
Mansperger, Julie Yates Mayfield, Softing Val, Diana
Smith Omeara, Lisa Easterling, Risdon Dean Reynolds,
Robert DeBlanc, Michele Crawford, Ulli Smith, Niki
Hurst, Ginny Dorrington, Jennifer Coleman, Tim Gwin,
Susan Pritchard, Linda Raines, Beth Bridges, Stephanie
Weill Andrew, Toni McNulty, Linus Hollis, Mike Sargent,
JaCinda Barnes, MJ Riemann, Sharon Dobson Schofield,
Barbara Cameron Slaton, Jayme Levy Duva, Abby Reyes
Gak, Renuka Pullat, Vicki Thomson, James Hall, Michele
Marie Heck Caskey, Susan Colgate, Jill McGraw
Lindeman, Sahara Ford-Davis, Laura Goodwin Kabel,
Sara Lemmon Pickard, Vicky Anderson, Jessica Harsin,
Heather Sturm, Leah Leah, Diane Mallon, Rose Buteau,
Sue Witten, Jeanne Kavanaugh, Teresa Howard, Lois
Adelman, Dawn Buege, Lisa Armstrong, Jinnie Grigsby,
Mitzi Martin Evans, Nadia Hicks, Steve Curtis, Celia
Kane, Rose Marie Sand, Dee Reames, Katina Marie, Ann
Mitchell Norman, Camille Thackston, Rebecca Pierce,
Kylie Thomson, Leigh Rademacher Cheloha, Pam
Kanthor, Catherine Jampel, Shannon Richner, Kristi
Strange, Casey Woodbury, Marjorie Young, Karen
Anderson, Jean Crawshaw, Shar L Jones, Kim Stokes-

Holder, Linda Marie, Jeff Collins, Kelly Reid, لــيلى جـــمال الـــديـــن, Kelly M. Paschal, Peggy Fowler Petrie, Claudia Villegas Ford, Marcy Volk, Melva Jeter, Sara McGhee Simons, Donna Odom Fournier, Beth Candelore, Kris Sandstrom, Colleen Scott, Susan Wodka, Susan Wodka, Jim Stroeher, Mark A Hope, Ryan Demers, John Davies, Tonya Bethley Hudson, Jamie Disch, Joyce Fagan Lindsay, Danielle Keister, Ross Youngblood, Chuck Murphy, Laura Flynn Hess, Duncan Koller, Christian Bell, Melissa A Graham, Ski Brush, Jacqui Olien, Louise Bellotti, Gayle Baker, Edna Alvarez-Rodgers, Lara Martinez, Shan Lee, Alexandria Wyeth, Patti DeCray, Karen Apelskog Torres, Lane Koeslin, Heike Kelley, Dacia Caglin, Anthoni M Bennett, Vikki Forsberg Bayton, Michael Gallipo, Tobi Raymond-Sparks, Jan Kellerman Marshall, Amy Jensen, Margaret Leafe, Christine Melcher, Maureen Kelly, Pam Fowler, Laura Koski, Terry Johnston, Amy Korn, Nancy Fawcett, Maggie G'Sell Gonzalez, Andi Irsik, Nena Cárdenas Freytag, Angela Freberg, Debbie Maria McCarrick, Nanaruth Carpenter, Margi Dickson Andrulonis, Kirby Nave, Nan Thornburg, Janet Marinaccio, Lana Angel, Susan Marks, Anne Larkin, Michael Braley, Pat Walden, Mellissa Minich, Alba Toro, Camala Ann Richardson, Giovanna McCarthy, Mark Ryan, Stacey Schoonmaker Hooper, Dan Shoemaker, Renee Lynn Flansburg, Rob Thompson, Debbie Patla Van Buren, Valerie Clark Melbrod, Shelby Jackowski-Walcher, Greg Cox, Daniel Levy, Randy George, Wil Morse, Arielle Ysabel Matic Mendoza, Sue Younglove, John Lemanski, Nick Masi, Geni Trotter, Rocco Galimi, Patty Keenan Hager, Mark Boardman, Lisa Hall, April

3

Zachary, Allen Peters, Kristy Rae, Robert Shea, Mary Pat Alberts Sprague, Jorge Bermudez, Barbara Thompson Budziak Browning, Geoff Bailie, Michael R. Hicks, Larry Irvin, Darcy Allison, Jo Ann Zawatski, Leah Adams, Diane Schmid McCall, John Fisher, Kristina Bua Horneck, Leslie M. Liggins-Wilder, David Shuman, Julie Cecile, Dave Strawn, Sarah Robinson, John Sandlin, Angelica Perry, Megan Wilcoxson, Jeremiah Kirch, Theresa Rakowski Polachek, Galina Capo, Bill Hubauer, Reidar Hansen, Greg Fife, Autumn Ross, Chris Homa, John Mueller, Kimberly Komnath Ellis, Bethany Thomas, Jane Schwartz Scelta, Joseph T. Buscaglia, Jennifer Anderson Moore, Mary DeMauro Barraco, James C Trotter, and Wayne Donaleski.

Thank you for all your wonderful comments. I do this for all of you.

MORNING

The soft edge of the bed sheet was like a warm kiss on his cheek. Through the slits of his eyelids he could see that the sun was already up, beams dancing across the bed through the sheer lace draperies that his wife had taken such care in making. The aroma of frying bacon wafted into the room, energizing his senses and causing his stomach to growl.

He rolled onto his back and stretched his arms above his head, letting the new day flow into his body. Out of the corner of his eye, he glimpsed soft blonde curls and half of a smiling face full of love peeking out around the door frame.

"I see you," he said, the first words of the day spoken to the one person on earth whom he loved more than life itself.

The girl's eyes lit up and her face broke into an even wider grin. She bounded across the room and leapt into the bed, draping her arms across her father's chest and nuzzling her head under his chin.

Kendrick Pryce kissed his daughter Maddie's forehead,

whispering, "Good morning, Sunshine. This is the best way to wake up."

Maddie squealed with joy and squeezed her father even tighter. Then she sat up, declaring, "Mom said breakfast is ready. You need to come quick before Papa eats all the bacon."

"Then I guess we'd better hurry," Ken nodded and, rising from the bed, he set off downstairs after his daughter.

Moments later he was kissing his wife Leanne as she handed him a steaming cup of coffee. "I thought you'd be up and working the upper fifty this morning."

"It's not going anywhere," he said with a grin. He sipped the coffee and let out an involuntary purr of satisfaction.

"It's also not gonna harvest itself," added Ken's father-in-law as he reached for another piece of bacon from the plate in the center of the table.

"Good morning to you, too, Will," Ken quipped with a wry smile.

"Dad, leave some bacon for Ken," his wife pleaded.

"Rumpelstiltskin shouldn't get any bacon. He hasn't done his chores yet."

Maddie enjoyed watching the daily banter between her father and grandfather. She knew that for all the bluster the two men loved and respected each other.

"Will, I might need your help bringing in the rest of the crop before the weekend. I want to make sure we get it over to the co-op by Friday afternoon."

The older man looked up from his eggs and replied, "You know this whole operation would be a lot easier if you'd invest in some automation. This organic farming business was novel for a while, but you're wasting perfectly good land and your precious time working it like a pioneer."

Ken glanced at his wife, her raised eyebrow cautioning him not to take the bait. "We've had this conversation a million times. Do we really need to have it again?"

Wiping his mouth with the cloth napkin, the elder went on, "Yes, we do. Look, Ken, it was fine when it was just you and Leanne, but you have bigger responsibilities now. You need to think of the future. You've got some prime land here. I've talked to the guy from AgroMax and he said…"

"Damn it, Will!"

Maddie and Leanne stiffened at Ken's sudden change in tone.

Lowering his voice, he continued, "I'm not going to turn my land into another corporate laboratory for genetically modified crops planted and harvested by robots." He gestured around the room and said, "All this is not about farming. It's about doing something *real*. Something meaningful with my own hands. It's about showing my child that there is joy and contentment in simplicity."

Will stared at him from across the table, shaking his head almost imperceptibly in disapproval. "And how is *all of this* preparing her for the world *out there*?"

"Just like the upper fifty, the world *out there* will always be *there*. Maddie will meet it on her own terms, but at least she'll have had *all this* to ground her."

Leanne reached over and placed her hand on Ken's, giving him her silent approval and gratitude for the life that they had built together.

PHOTOS

Leanne muted the television and called toward the den, "Ken, you're exhausted. You really should come and relax." She paused, waiting for a reply, and then added a special enticement with a playful lilt in her voice, "I'll make popcorn."

Ken leaned back in his desk chair, stretched, and then rubbed his burning eyes. Frowning at the screen full of weather data, crop yield projections, and irrigation maps, he knew he had to quit. It would be fruitless to continue working when his heart was not in it.

Standing up, he walked to the door of the den and snapped off the light. He crossed the room and stood behind the sofa placing his hands on his wife's shoulders. Leanne reached up and covered his rough hands with hers.

"Come sit down," she said, patting the cushion beside her.

Ken walked around the sofa and collapsed into the soft leather. Allowing himself to be engulfed in Leanne's embrace, he leaned his head on her chest and drank in her familiar scent—a swirl of her favorite perfume with a hint of laundry detergent.

"You know you don't have to work so hard," she whispered. "We could hire another hand so that you can spend more time in the office."

"I'd rather be out in the fields. You know I hate staring at that damned screen."

"Then why don't we get someone to do the office work?" She stroked his hair and Ken closed his eyes. "You know my dad would gladly…"

He cut her off gently, "Your father thinks I'm wasting my life. I have to hear about how I'm not taking care of my family every time he helps out. Besides, I don't need him poking around in our books. He doesn't need to know that we're not exactly getting rich with this place."

"He's just worried about us, that's all." She gently moved his head from her chest and took his face in her hands. "You know I wouldn't trade our life for any amount of money."

Ken gazed into her sparkling blue eyes and knew that she meant the words but didn't always enjoy the struggle. "I know. I just can't help but wonder if we've made the right choices for Maddie. She's growing up in a world that's changing so fast. It's like we live on an island of sanity in a world gone completely mad."

"We do." She smiled gently, "It's an island that *you* created for us. This house, this farm, our family—you're the one that convinced me that Maddie needed a life rooted in the things that truly matter."

Ken sighed and sat up to peer absently into his lap. Leanne, meanwhile, rose from the sofa. Crossing the room, she opened a drawer in an antique roll top desk and retrieved from it a large leather photo album. Then she returned to the couch and gently opened the cover of the book, letting it rest across her knees.

Pointing to a photograph on the first page, Leanne glanced at Ken.

"It's right here, babe," she said, tapping on the picture. "That's the moment when I knew life with you was going to be an adventure."

Ken's brow furrowed.

"Why that particular moment?" he asked.

"Think about it, silly. Who brings an old-fashioned film camera on a first date? I thought to myself 'this guy is super-romantic but a little odd'. But after like the fifth date I realized that you're really just a man lost in time. You try to be a part of this world, but you really belong in some other world from a long time ago. The good news for you is that I find that strangely interesting and sexy as hell."

Ken blushed. "People think I'm weird, always snapping away with my old Nikon. I believe some things just don't need to be improved on."

Leanne continued flipping through the pages of the photo album, smiling as she relived the tender moments of their early years—the trips, parties, and other candid moments around the house. A tear formed in her eye as she scanned the pages with the photos of their newborn daughter—her first birthday party, laughing in her father's lap on the tractor as a toddler, and catching her first fish at the age of three.

Wiping a tear from her eye, Leanne said quietly, "Thank you, Ken."

"For taking so many pictures?"

"No. For making our lives worth remembering."

Ken leaned over and kissed Leanne on the cheek. "I thought you were going to make popcorn."

FISHING

The morning sun crested the horizon just as Ken and Maddie arrived at the small lake which bordered the north side of their farm. He adjusted the small backpack of food on his shoulder and breathed deeply of the crisp morning air. A smile formed on his face. How on earth could he have second-guessed the wisdom of moving to this place? No cityscape could surpass its pastoral beauty. Quiet and still, the countryside filled him with a sublime sense of contentment. The serenity alone was worth struggling for in an era increasingly detached from the natural world.

Maddie walked next to him swinging her tackle box. He noticed that she was rapidly becoming a young woman and could now match his stride. It occurred to him that she would soon prefer to spend hours with her girlfriends doing the things teenage girls like to do rather than spend time casting for perch and yellow bass with her father. All the more reason to cherish these moments and lock them away for the years when such memories would be his only companion.

A blanket of mist hung over the lake, enhancing the

dreamlike quality of the scene. Maddie's hair hung in loose long curls over her shoulders. Her beautiful face, a sprinkle of freckles across her nose, was alive and glowed in the rays of the gently rising sun.

Ken was both grateful and fearful as he realized time was accelerating and his daughter was gradually being pulled into a new orbit. One that would take her into high school then university, and then to a new life with new people, and inexorably away from her parents. It was a natural progression—of that he was keenly aware—but he pushed against it and struggled to keep time at bay for just a little while. Perhaps until they could catch just a few more fish together.

After they each enjoyed an apple and a slice of Leanne's scrumptious banana bread, the two sat quietly, casting and carefully jigging their lures through the still water. Maddie was a serious fisherman and approached the whole affair with a calmness and resolve that impressed her father. She almost always caught more fish than Ken, and he delighted in her intensity as she reeled in one fish after another. He loved the way she would bite her lower lip and knit her eyebrows with the ardor of a professional angler. Such determination was a trait that he hoped would serve her well in life.

Maddie set her pole aside for a moment and picked up her cup, taking a sip of the now tepid coffee. She asked without warning, "Dad, why did you decide to become a farmer?"

Of the thousands of questions that Maddie had posed to him over the years, this was the one that he had feared the most. Not because of any shame associated with his chosen path, but because of the emotions those memories stirred up.

"Well, I guess it seemed like the thing I was best suited for," he responded, not altogether convincingly.

"Dad, you were an astronaut. How does someone go from astronaut to farmer?"

"Actually, I was a geologist who just happened to get a perfect score on the Space Sciences Aptitude Test. The recruiters back in those days were very good at selling the dream of 'humanity's next great chapter' in space. I had prepared myself for a life of digging rocks and staring into a microscope, but they sold me pretty hard on what I could do *out there*."

"But still, you signed up. Why didn't you go back after the accident?"

Ken looked out across the lake searching for something to say but decided the truth was all he could offer. "I suppose it's because I was never truly committed. I loved the people…my God…they were the most amazing people. Better than me in every way and still, we were friends. Real friends. The kind that you don't just find, but instead, the kind that you earn." He drew in a breath, sighed and continued, "After the accident I realized that without my team, there was no reason for me to go back. I didn't want to go because of the work. I only wanted to go because they would be with me and they would make the work meaningful. Do you understand?"

Maddie searched her father's face for a long moment, her eyes locked onto his. "I think so." She set down the coffee cup and picked up her pole. "I hope I can earn friends like them some day."

Ken put his arm around Maddie and drew her close to him. "I have no doubt that you will."

After casting her line, she asked, "So, why farming?"

Ken fell silent for a moment before looking over at his daughter. "I remember one summer when I was about fifteen. My parents dragged me out to a wedding of some distant cousin. It was a barn wedding at this farm out near DeKalb. We got there early in the morning to help set up the decorations and all that. I must have looked like a typical miserable teenager so the guy who owned the farm came over to me and said, 'Hey kid. You ever drive a tractor?' I told him that I'd never even seen one up close. Five minutes later I was driving this gigantic tractor across a field and I was hooked. Then the farmer took me across the road and told me way too much about corn. We picked a bunch and put it in the trunk of my parents' car to take home. I remember thinking that this guy really loved what he does."

"So why did you go to college and do geology when you knew that farming was your dream?"

The question caused Ken to sit up straight and ponder his choice for the first time in nearly thirty years. "Well...I suppose it's because I wasn't really pursuing my dream, but rather my parent's dream for me." He chuckled and continued, "Going to college wasn't optional in my family. Your grandparents both have advanced degrees and they believe that education is the key to purpose and fulfillment."

Maddie titled her head and regarded her father through squinted eyes, "But you don't believe that. Mom doesn't either. You've always told me that I should follow my heart."

"That's right. I guess you've been listening." He smiled broadly at his daughter, his heart filled with pride. "So what do you want to do? You know…after high school?"

"Assuming I totally crush eighth grade," she joked, "and I graduate high school, I guess I'd like to work in an exotic place. You know, somewhere far away."

"You mean like Sioux City?"

The girl rolled her eyes as only adolescent girls can. "Dad…you're so funny. No, like…I don't know…Africa or maybe Indonesia. I know that I want to help people. I'm just not sure how yet."

Ken smiled and said, "You've got time to figure it out. And remember that you don't have to pick one thing. You can be passionate about a bunch of things and work on all of them. You're going to have a long and interesting lifetime to chase your dreams."

"Right now, I'm passionate about some more of that banana bread," Maddie quipped.

"You get us another fish and I'll get us some more banana bread."

Maddie slung the pole quickly over her shoulder and with a flick of her wrist, expertly cast the lure to a spot near a log.

Ken paused for a moment and drank in the vision of Maddie with her fishing pole, her curls bouncing in the breeze, and the future alight in her eyes. For all the mistakes and failures in his life he knew he had atoned, and in that place, he realized he was truly content.

SOLO

Ken and Leanne stood in front of the hangar on a frosty morning in November. Each wore a unique expression of concern mixed with anticipation. Today, the weekly lessons and endless hours of study would culminate in Maddie becoming a certified and licensed pilot under the supervision of her instructor, a decorated former military pilot and astronaut, who just happened to also be her grandfather.

As the single-engine plane came around and lined up with the runway, Leanne said, "Oh my God, Ken. I can't watch." She clutched his right arm tightly.

He moved the camera from his eye and said, "Honey, you're gonna make me miss the shot."

Leanne gave him an embarrassed look and said, "Sorry. I don't know why I'm so nervous. I've watched her land dozens of times." She glanced over her shoulder to the small tower and caught Will's eye as he lowered the binoculars. He gave her a vigorous 'thumbs up' and she smiled and returned the gesture.

"She's got this. Right, Ken? She's got this."

Ken was busy firing off shots of the small plane with his trusty old Nikon. Just as the plane touched down he shouted, "Yeah! That's my girl!"

He turned to Leanne and noted her gloved hands clapping excitedly, tears streaming down her face.

"Are you crying?" Ken asked.

She wiped her eyes and said, "Shut up. Did you get some good pictures?"

"You're damned right I did."

The plane slowly made its way down the taxiway to halt near where Ken and Leanne stood. Will ran down the steps of the tower and across the tarmac before halting, out of breath and hands on his knees, beside the plane while the propeller fluttered to a halt.

Maddie pushed open the bubble canopy of the small plane and raised her arms in a triumphant salute to her grandfather. The old astronaut held her headset as she climbed out of the cockpit. She turned and hugged her grandfather and said, "Thank you, Papa. That was amazing!"

Will held his granddaughter and said, "You were perfect. Like a steely-eyed missile man. Now go see you your mother before she falls apart."

Maddie glided over to her mother's waiting arms and let out a strained, "Okay, Mom. Ease up on the grip a little."

Leanne opened her mouth and the anxiety tumbled out as, "That was incredible! Oh my God…I can't believe how nervous I was. I mean I've seen you fly dozens of times, but that…well…that was amazing! Was it scary? You know…flying all by yourself."

Maddie glanced past her mother and saw her dad in his

usual pose at moments like this—pointing the old Nikon at her capturing a shot for his treasured photo album.

Through the lens, Ken saw Maddie look directly at him, a mischievous grin on her lips, and as he pressed the shutter release, she gave him her trademark wink.

Later that evening Ken emerged from the old converted pantry that served as his darkroom.

Will was seated at the kitchen table reading a book, his glasses perched on the end of his nose. He looked up when he heard the darkroom door open and gave Ken his usual glare of disapproval. "Get some good shots today?"

Ken was surprised by the question and tone of genuine interest. "Yeah. I got a perfect shot of her touching down with the front wheel up and a big smile on her face."

"She's a really good pilot, Ken. I hope you know that."

Ken pulled out a chair and sat down. "Well, she had a great instructor."

"I'm just a rusty old missile man. It's a wonder you let me drive a tractor."

"You know you made my little girl very happy today, Will. Thanks for that."

Will dismissed the comment with a wave of his hand. "She's no little girl anymore, Ken. She's sixteen and smarter than any of us. She's got unlimited potential."

Ken sat up with his hands spread out on the old wooden table, "Is this the part where you tell me how I'm keeping her from reaching her potential by…"

Will cut him off, "Damn it, Ken. That's not what I was going to say."

"No? All her life you've been telling me how this lifestyle is limiting her. I just wish you'd accept that this is our life. We get to choose how we live and how we raise our daughter."

Will shook his head and began to laugh. "You know, Ken…you're a thick son-of-a-bitch. Is that what you've been thinking all these years? That I'm judging you and Leanne for choosing to live on a farm in the middle of Iowa?"

Ken was confused. He looked across the table and saw a look in his father-in-law's eyes he had never seen before. It was a look of empathy and pain. "Well…it seems that way."

"Is it news to you that I'm a crusty old bastard? For Christ's sake, Ken. I spent the first fifteen years of my life flying fighters in combat zones all over the world and the next fifteen years flying gear, fuel, and colonists back and forth to Mars. Who the hell am I to judge how a man runs his family?" The old man's eyes remained fixed on Ken, almost pleading to be understood.

Ken wondered if he had misunderstood the man all these years.

"I was a terrible father, Ken. I was gone for every single important moment of Leanne's life. I missed her birth, nearly every birthday, graduation, school plays, thousands of dinners, story time, lazy days around the house. I wasn't present for any of it. Christ, I blinked and suddenly she was twenty-eight and marrying some former geologist-astronaut who wanted to be a farmer. Every day, I'm still getting to know her. Earning her trust, showing her that I love her. Trying to make up for being a shitty father."

It was the most emotion Ken had ever witnessed from his father-in-law. "She loves you very, very much, Will. I hope you know that."

Will's eyes welled up with tears and the words stuck in

his throat. He just waved the comment away.

"And Maddie. My God, Will. She absolutely worships the ground you walk on. And it makes me very happy and grateful to see how well you love my daughter."

The tears overflowed the old man's rheumy eyes and ran in the creases of his rugged face. He wiped his eyes quickly on the sleeve of his flannel shirt, leaned over the table and pointed a finger at Ken. "You listen to me. You've done something that is worth more than every goddamned medal on my old uniform, or any bank account, or any of that shit. You've made a life. A real life. You have a wife that loves you. You've raised an incredible daughter who is going to shock all of us with her greatness someday. And you've made a home that's full of love. That's enough accomplishment for a lifetime. So stop comparing yourself to me or to what you thought you were going to be."

The words stunned Ken. Will had never displayed this level of emotion in front him before and it was unsettling to see the man cry. He was glad that Leanne and Maddie weren't around to witness this unprecedented crack in the man's gruff facade. He suspected that Will was also thankful for the rare moment of privacy.

"So, basically you're saying that you're proud of me and that you love me," Ken teased.

Will shook his head and said with his best faux scowl, "You're not half the asshole I thought you were when Leanne first brought you around. Let's leave it at that."

The two men regarded one another from across the table and across the years and, after a moment, they laughed.

GRADUATION

The day of Maddie's high school graduation came as a shock to Ken and Leanne. It seemed to them just yesterday that the girl was swinging in the yard, climbing trees, and swimming in the pond with her friends.

Sitting in the blazing Iowa sun with the scores of other parents, Ken couldn't help but wonder if all the choices he had made for his family had yielded the best possible life for them. Would Maddie be disadvantaged at university having grown up on a 'museum farm', as the kids called it? Would she be equipped for the world that awaited her far from rural Iowa? *Does she already resent the life I chose for her?* he wondered.

Leanne dabbed a tear from her eye as she leaned into her husband. "Look…she's next."

Maddie strode across the platform, her yellow graduation gown flowing in the summer breeze, her head held high, eyes fixed on the future. She shook the hand of her principal as he handed her the rolled diploma tied with a green and yellow ribbon. She glanced over her shoulder and caught her father's eye, giving him the playful wink he cherished.

The graduation party was well attended by family from as far away as Chicago and St. Louis, dozens of Maddie's friends from school, and a handful of neighbors, local business owners, and the guys from the John Deere dealership.

Ken spent much of the afternoon in front of the grill turning out a seemingly endless stream of hamburgers and hot dogs. Leanne circulated through the crowd offering refreshments and keeping the side dishes replenished. Will kept the men and a few of Maddie's male classmates entertained with tales of his days as a pilot on colonial ships headed for Mars. He enjoyed his status as a local hero and one of the very few people from this part of Iowa to journey off-planet, even in a world where space travel was becoming more and more commonplace.

Every few minutes Ken would glance across the yard to catch a glimpse of Maddie laughing and posing for pictures with her friends. He smiled at the young man who shadowed her every movement as she gracefully circulated from group to group giving each person in attendance a hug and her sincere thanks for helping her celebrate the day. The young man had an enraptured glow around him that told Ken that he was probably in love with Maddie, and that he needed to keep an eye on the boy. In that moment, he glanced over at Leanne and recalled how he felt whenever he was near her in those early days of fluttering stomachs and sweaty palms. "God, she still looks amazing," he whispered to himself.

That evening after the guests had departed and the evidence of the party had been cleared from the yard,

Ken reclined in his favorite wicker rocker on the broad old porch listening to the crickets and watching the fireflies dance on the silent evening breeze. He sipped an ice-cold beer and let the events of the day wash over him.

The screen door creaked open and as he turned he saw Maddie silhouetted in the light from the kitchen.

"Hey…mind if I join you?" she asked.

He grabbed the arm of the other rocker and pulled it close and replied, "Come sit and talk to your old man."

Maddie sat down and took her father's hand and said, "I just want to thank you for the party. Everyone had a great time."

"You mean your friends didn't mind that we didn't throw a keg party for you?"

"C'mon, Dad. Everyone knows that Colton's parents always have the best keg parties." She winked. "They come here for the food and Papa's stories."

"He's quite the entertainer," he said with a hint of sarcasm.

Maddie let the comment hang in the air, not wanting to ruin the moment. She decided to change the subject. "Did you take some good pictures today?"

"You know I always do. Of course I'm going to have to do some editing."

Maddie gave him a quizzical look. "Why's that?"

"That Bjornbak boy was glued to you all day. He's in just about every shot—even some of the closeups."

"Kyle is just a friend, Dad. You *know* that."

"Sure, I know that. But does he?"

"Trust me. I've made it perfectly clear." She shifted in her seat telegraphing her discomfort with the topic.

"You forget, I was a young man once. What I saw today

was a guy in love with my baby girl. I just want to know that he's a good guy."

Maddie leaned forward and cocked her head in that familiar way that told Ken she was serious. "We're not having this conversation. He's just a friend."

Ken put his hands up in mock surrender, "Okay, okay. He's just a friend." He paused with a smirk lingering on his lips. "A friend who's completely gaga for my girl. I just want to know if I should start planning a wedding with your mother. We proved we can throw a helluva party."

Maddie shook her head and said through a wide grin, "You're so ridiculous."

They both laughed easily and then paused to let the evening breeze wash over them.

"I actually came out here to have a serious conversation with you."

Ken raised an eyebrow and said, "Maybe I should trade this beer in for something stronger."

"Relax. It's not bad—just, you know, serious."

"Okay…what is it?"

"Well…I've been thinking about my plans for this fall. I know we're all set for me to go to Chicago, but I've been thinking about another option."

Ken sat up straight, a pit growing in his stomach, "What other option?"

"I know you and mom opted me out of the SSAT, but I thought about it and decided to take it anyway. I got a nearly perfect score."

"What? Why would you do that?" Ken could feel his neck and ears turning red.

"Now, Dad…don't get upset…"

"I'm not upset. But I'd like to know why you felt the

need to hide this from us."

Maddie took a deep breath and continued, "Well, I know how you feel about that lifestyle. And I don't want you blaming Papa…"

"Really? I do blame him for filling your head with all that garbage about space ships and the life out there."

"Dad, I'm not talking about spending my life shuttling back and forth between Earth and Mars. There's so much more that my generation can do. We need to think beyond what we can grab for ourselves. I want my life to mean something."

The words struck Ken like an arrow in the heart. For the past eighteen years he had dreaded the day when his daughter would see the world beyond the farm, beyond the county and it's endless fields of corn and soybeans, past the wind turbines, and into the infinite blackness of space. He strained against the pull that humanity's greatest adventure had on the mind of his beloved daughter.

He understood all too well how powerful a force it was. He too, like his father-in-law, had once stood on the platform, looking up at the rocket that would take him to orbit and on to a frozen and lifeless world waiting to be transformed. The dream of space and all it held for humanity had captured his mind and put his life on a trajectory that would end in disaster for eleven men and women he called his friends and colleagues. The years of training could never have prepared him for the death of his friends and of his dream in a single flash.

"What do you mean? You want to work on the ground in support or flight operations? Maybe an engineering specialty? They always need good engineers and you're brilliant in math."

"No, Dad." Maddie took her father's hand again and said, "I've applied for a colonial mission."

The words struck Ken like a punch in the chest. He slumped back in the chair, his face slack and mouth open. He wanted to scream but knew that this was one of those moments that would define his relationship with his daughter from this day forward.

"Why?" was all he dared utter.

Maddie gazed out across the yard and smiled at the fireflies, almost envying their freedom and the beauty of their singular purpose. "Because you and Mom taught me to seek meaning in everything I do."

To hear his own sentiment spoken back at him by his precious one jarred him more deeply than he could have imagined. Ken closed his eyes, then let out a long and mournful breath. He whispered to his precious one, "I know."

DEPARTURE

Ken entered the kitchen and found Leanne sitting at the table, a half empty cup of coffee in front of her. Her gaze fixed on nothing in particular, anxiously wringing her hands. She didn't turn when Ken said, "How you doing?"

He let the question hang in the air and went to the counter and poured a cup of coffee. The sound of Ken putting the pot back on the counter snapped Leanne out of her fugue state.

She turned and said, "What? Did you say something?"

He sat down across from her at the table and replied, "I just asked how you're doing."

Leanne opened her mouth to speak but the words caught in her throat.

"It's okay to cry, you know," Ken said gently.

Shaking her head, she replied forcefully, "No, it's not. This day isn't about me or you. It's Maddie's day. She's starting her life today. We can't rob her of a great memory with a lot of tears and selfish emotion." She wiped her eyes quickly. "I won't do that to her. She's worked too hard."

"Then we put on our brave faces and send her off with a smile." Ken nodded his head in an effort to convince himself of the wisdom of the plan. "I can do that."

Leanne reached over and took Ken's hand, her face suddenly gentle and almost pleading. "I need you to do me a favor today."

Ken's eyes widened and he said, "Of course. What?"

"I need you to not be 'Mr. Memory-Maker' today. Can you do that for me?"

The request shocked Ken. But he easily read the signs in his wife's face and knew this wasn't really a request. "Sure. It'll be nice to just be part of the action for a change."

She cocked her head and raised an eyebrow and said, "You so don't mean that but it's nice of you to play along."

Suddenly from upstairs Maddie shouted, "Hey, Dad! Can you come help me with my bags?"

Ken took a gulp of his coffee and replied with a reassuring smile to Leanne, "On my way!"

Later that morning after a breakfast that highlighted all of Maddie's favorites—French toast, thick-cut smoked bacon, cinnamon apple turnover pancake, fresh squeezed orange juice, and cantaloupe—the family gathered in the driveway to say goodbye.

Maddie was wearing a pair of denim cutoffs, a blue tank top, and her signature red bandanna tying her golden hair into a messy ponytail. She was tan from a long summer of training runs and swimming with her friends. Many of her classmates had already departed for university and she had spent the last few days packing and gathering last minute items for her long drive to

California.

The last of the bags were put into the trunk of her battered old Tesla Riva while Will checked the status of the solar paneled surface of the old vehicle. He looked up from his data pad and announced, "I managed to increase the panel efficiency to twenty-eight percent. That's as good as it's gonna get for this old rust bucket."

Maddie smiled at the old man and said, "Thanks, Papa. Now I won't have to stop to recharge hardly at all."

He nodded his approval.

"Well…I really should get on the road. It's a long drive." Maddie stood next to the car looking at her parents and grandfather. She saw the farm house and the yard and the endless rows of corn beyond and realized that everything that she cared about in the world was right in front of her, filling her eyes, burning into her memory.

"I had a bunch of stuff I wanted to say to each of you, but I just couldn't get it all sorted out in my head. Maybe I'll take some time and write it all down. I don't know…"

Ken spoke up and said, "You just focus on what's in front of you, not what's behind."

Maddie titled her head in the way she always did and said, "But, Dad…I *am* focused on what's in front of me. I just need you—all of you—to know that I love you and I wouldn't trade a day of the life I've had."

She stepped over to her grandfather and was immediately engulfed in his thick arms. She said quietly into his ear, "Thank you for letting me fly." She kissed his stubbly cheek and added just above a whisper, "You're my favorite steely-eyed missile man."

Will squeezed her tightly and managed to croak out, "Your Papa loves you and will miss you very much." He then released her and headed for the house, his steps burdened by the tears he was holding back.

Leanne's dam of calm finally broke and she grabbed Maddie in a tight embrace and said, "You go and be great. We're always here, no matter what." Her voice thick with emotion she added, "I love you, Bug."

"I love you to, Mom. Thank you for showing me what a strong woman is. I hope I can be like you for myself and maybe for a husband some day."

Leanne just nodded then kissed Maddie three times, as she had since the day she was born.

Finally, Maddie stepped in front of her father, her hands jammed into her pockets. "I know you're not okay with this." Ken began to speak and she shook her head and continued, "It's alright, Dad. I don't blame you. You of all people have a right to question my choice. But I also know that you understand in here," she took a hand from her pocket and pointed to his heart, "why I'm doing this. And that a little piece of you wishes you had gone *out there*."

Ken opened his arms and his little girl stepped into the place that made her feel safe for as long as she could remember. "You're my world. I'll miss you more than you can know."

After a long embrace, Ken dug into his pocket and pulled out a small foil pouch. He took Maddie's hand and placed the pouch into her palm.

"What's this?" she asked.

"Seeds. I thought maybe you could plant a little piece of home out there."

Maddie closed her hand around the precious seeds and tucked them into her pocket. "Thanks, Dad."

"Well…I'd better hit the road." Maddie gave her mother and father one more quick hug, got into the car, and drove down the long driveway and turned west toward Interstate 80 leading across the Missouri River to Omaha and beyond.

Will watched from the porch with Ken's old Nikon hanging around his neck, his face moist with tears.

BEACH

Ken dug his toes into the warm sand and drank in the salty Pacific breeze. He noted that the sun felt different in California—less harsh, and more invigorating. The Iowa sun was unforgiving by comparison, dusty and oppressive as it illuminated his daily efforts. But here he felt lighter, more alive, his mind free of the clutter and lists of things to be done. In this moment there was just now; the sand, the sun, and the waves. As if it all existed just for him.

The sound of laughter from somewhere behind Ken made him turn toward the dunes. He watched as the dune buggy crested the hill and stopped, Maddie's hair flying around her face. Will's mouth was open in an expression of adrenaline-fueled delight from the passenger seat. The two waved and Maddie shouted, "We're going to make one more run, then we'll eat!"

Ken waved and replied, "Sounds good!"

Maddie mashed the accelerator and sped the buggy down the dune and then up the side of the next hill, getting all four wheels off the ground. The sound of their laughter drifting behind carried away by the breeze.

Leanne approached with a handful of tiny seashells. She placed them gently on the blanket and sat down next to her husband. "Dad is having way too much fun."

"He's the youngest octogenarian I've ever seen. I hope I'm still riding the dunes when I'm his age."

Leanne smiled and jibed, "I think a tractor is all the excitement you can handle."

Ken mindlessly shuffled through the collection of sea shells with his finger.

Leanne asked, "Are you ready for this?"

He shook his head. "Not in the least. I just can't wrap my head around the fact that I'll never hold her in my arms again after tomorrow. It's like she's…"

Leanne cut him off abruptly, "Don't say it, Ken!"

He reached over and caressed her arm. "I'm sorry. But that's what it feels like."

"We'll have the video messages. That's something."

"But we'll never have a real conversation with her again." Ken paused and let the wave of welling tears pass. "I just didn't expect to feel this empty."

"You never know. I was reading that they're working on a return option. It may be years away, but surely they'll need to make returns a reality. They can't expect everyone to make a one-way trip."

Ken attempted a reassuring smile but only managed a piteous grimace. "The only return ticket right now is incapacity or madness."

She put her hand to her mouth. "It's funny. In these five years of her training and all those moments of worry and sadness, I never once considered that she might fail at this." Leanne put her hand on Ken's back and said, "She's going to do great things, Ken. We have no reason to be anything but proud and thankful. We made an amazing human being."

He put his arm around Leanne and raised his eye to a spot down the beach. "Here they come. Let's get the food ready."

Later, after they had finished eating Ken asked Maddie, "Is there anything else you'd like to do today before we get you back to base?"

"I only have one item left on my bucket list."

Leanne asked, "Your what?"

Will answered, "Her bucket list. Stuff she wants to do before she 'kicks the bucket'."

"Jesus, Dad! She's not dying," Leanne exclaimed. Turning to Maddie, "Why would you make such a morbid list…"

"Mom! Take a breath. It's just an old expression. I made a list of things I wanted to experience before I leave. I've been working on it for more than four years." She shrugged and said, "I thought I mentioned it."

Ken looked at Leanne silently urging her to lighten the sudden tension. She must have received his telepathic caution as she said, "Of course you did. That makes perfect sense. I'm sorry…I just never heard…"

Leanne lowered her eyes and smiled at her mother. "Mom. It's fine. I've actually had an amazing time doing some really neat stuff. Half of it I probably never would've done if not for the mission. So, I look at it like I'm squeezing every drop of awesome out of this life before I start a new one."

Ken and Will exchanged a proud look.

"So, what's the one thing you have left to do?" Ken asked again.

Maddie cocked her head in the way her father loved then stood up extending a hand to each of her parents. They glanced at each other and then, taking Maddie's hands, stood up. "I want to take a walk along the beach with my parents." She turned to her grandfather and said, "You don't mind, do you, Papa?"

Will waved off the comment, "I'm gonna relax and enjoy the sunset. You go."

The three walked hand-in-hand along the shoreline, the waves straining to erase their footprints against the falling tide. The sky was ablaze with layer upon layer of magenta, crimson, and tangerine clouds, like gaudy sheets of linen piled on the horizon. Will smiled as he watched them move down the strand and reflected on the immensity of the moment. The only three people he cared about in the whole world were spending the last moments they would ever share together in this life. His breath caught in his throat and he reached into the tattered leather case to lift Ken's old Nikon to his eye. The shutter clicked, preserving the silhouetted family against the giant dying sun.

LAUNCH

Ken and Leanne sat holding hands as Will squinted into the binoculars inspecting every inch of the giant rocket standing tall on the launchpad at Vandenberg Space Port. The goodbyes had been said and all that remained were the tears to be shed across the years to come.

The viewing gallery reserved for family and friends of the crew was packed with onlookers. Everyone wore an expression of anticipation mixed with sadness and tinged with fear. *It's too much*, thought Ken bitterly. *They expect us to sit here and cheer as we send our children away forever.*

To the left side of the viewing gallery stood a massive transparent display with the countdown clock steadily ticking off the seconds until launch. Across the bottom of the display a continuous crawl of the crew members smiling and hopeful faces followed by their names and mission specialties ran over and over. Ken had already watched Maddie's wide grin slide by three times while they waited. His mind automatically calculated the next time she would appear based on the one hundred crew members, the speed of the crawl across the display, and the display width. The countdown clock stood at 05:34 and he knew he would see Maddie's picture one more time before the launch.

For the past five years as Maddie progressed in her training, Ken had listened to her excitedly recount stories of survival training in Death Valley, wild zero-G flights, sky diving, rock climbing, piloting a wide variety of aircraft, and he had even watched her launch from this pad twice on training missions to the ISS-3 and the Lunar Colonial Training Academy at Peary Crater. He marveled at the way she mastered every task, and memorized every step of the multitude of complex jobs she was learning how to perform. It often took him back to his training, and it wrung his heart dry with the memories of his fallen comrades. But through it all, his sadness and dread for this day was always tempered by immense pride and satisfaction in knowing that Maddie was pursuing her dreams with every ounce of her being. She was happy, and that was all that mattered to Ken.

"The stage one fuel tank is venting. They should be shutting their visors about now," Will said loud enough for half the gallery to hear.

Leanne jabbed her elbow into Ken's rib excitedly, "Look! Oh, my god…they're showing the crew."

The main section of the giant display gave the gallery a bird's eye view of the interior of the spacecraft. The one hundred colonists were seated in ten descending sections of ten seats around the interior hull of the ship, all facing inward. The stark white decking and surface materials of the ship's interior appeared sterile and lifeless. The pale blue and green of the crew's flight suits offered the only color in the otherwise spartan scene. The lighting was such that no one's face could be seen through the helmet visors. For this, Ken was thankful.

Leanne clutched Ken's arm tightly. He could feel her trembling as she locked her eyes on the massive white rocket.

"Well, this is it," said Will, his voice now a mere whisper. His eyes welled up with tears as Leanne blindly reached for her father's hand, hoping to gain some measure of strength from his touch.

The staccato voice counting down the final seconds until launch seemed muffled as Ken focused the sum total of his being on the rocket, as if he could lift it to the heavens through the force of his will alone.

The flash came first, then the billowing white cloud erupted from the base of the rocket, growing faster and faster as the massive engines poured their fury against the earth. Slowly the giant white rocket rose gracefully, sliding past the launch tower, then finally into the steel blue sky, carried aloft by a ferocious furnace.

The shockwave rippled across the lagoon in front of the viewing gallery and struck the onlookers as they collectively released sounds of cries, cheers, laughter, and sobs. Maddie's family stood still, eyes fixed skyward, as a piece of their heart roared toward orbit.

EVENING

Ken cradled the photograph in his leathery hands and gently placed an adhesive tab over each corner of the photo. He carefully peeled the backing from each tab and positioned the photo over the lower right of the page. Once it was aligned perfectly he pressed each tab firmly with his dry and cracked thumb. He lay his hands on either side of the album and admired the latest entry in this, the most special of his many photo albums.

Leanne stopped behind his chair and remarked, "Can you believe how grey Maddie's hair is? I think she has more grey than I do."

"It's because of the fractional gravity. Does something to the...um...the hair...ahhh..."

"Follicles. Hair follicles, Ken."

"What? Oh, yes...follicles. I knew that." Ken smacked his lips and smiled at the photo of a middle-aged Maddie holding up an ear of corn with a broad smile and her signature wink.

"Damn fine job, Sunshine."

"It was nice to hear that the colony is doing so well.

She's so proud to finally have your corn growing. I think it's nice that she's taking a trip to the new station at Elysium. It must be wonderful to get above ground once in a while and see the open spaces."

Ken made to answer Leanne, but when he opened his mouth the breath would not come. Gasping, he stared down at Maddie's photo as it fell away from him. Walls of encroaching darkness closed in around Ken, sending him hurtling down a tunnel and as his head hit the table, he heard Leanne's voice scream from somewhere far away, "Ken! Oh my God, Ken!"

REALITY

Shadows. Gauzy fluttering things. Sounds. Flashes of lightning and concussions of sound in his brain. Cold. So cold. Air rushing over his skin.

I can feel.

Then a spasm struck his detached body. He was vaguely aware of the tension gripping every muscle, but he did not care. More light. Sounds becoming clearer.

I'm not dead.

From far away, as if down a long corridor muffled by the sounds of colossal machinery, grinding, whirring, buzzing as they spun and moved, he could hear a voice. The words were forming in his mind.

A name?

"Lieutenant Pryce. Sir. Can you hear me?" The voice was closer.

My name?

Unintelligible chattering. More lights. Shapes floating around him in the air. Something pressing into his skin but where on his body he could not say for sure.

Where am I?

"Lieutenant Pryce, you need to open your eyes and give me one good cough."

Having clearly understood, Ken decided to comply. He thought about coughing and found his body racked by another spasm followed by a gush of liquid erupting over his chest. Tears welled in his eyes and he was suddenly struck by a wave of nausea.

"Roll him to his side. Quickly, please. There you go, Lieutenant. You're doing just fine."

Another spasm and more wetness.

"Good job, Lieutenant Pryce. Okay. Now take a nice deep breath for me."

Ken felt hands roll him onto his back once again and now he could see the outlines and shapes of faces, eyes, and mouths hovering above him.

"My eyes," he managed to croak.

"Right. Let's turn down those lights for you, Lieutenant."

The glaring of the world subsided considerably and Ken's eyes began to clear as tears rolled into his ears.

"Let's clean you up a bit."

Hands moved some sort of fabric across his face, chest, and shoulders.

"Okay, now we're going to sit you up and you let us know if you feel uncomfortable."

The bed rose behind his head bringing his torso up to almost a sitting position. A mild wave of nausea rose then passed. He said, "I'm okay."

"Great. You gave us a little scare there, Lieutenant Pryce. You didn't want to wake up."

In a flash Ken realized where he was. The kitchen table and the farm and all that he loved began to fold in his mind like a pop-up story book. Vivid, colorful, and enchanting, but ultimately nothing more than cleverly cut paper and precision folds.

The two technicians recognized the signs. As their training prescribed they quietly excused themselves from the room and left Ken to sob alone on the bed.

OUTBOUND

Ken fastened the collar of his jacket as he stared at the impossibly young face in the mirror. He looked down at his hands and marveled at how he always felt so utterly foreign after a return. He knew the sensation would rapidly dissipate over the next few days, but it was always disconcerting and an unpleasant consequence of his chosen form of layover entertainment.

He ran his fingers through his astonishingly thick hair and smiled knowing that he still had four days to enjoy before returning to duty.

The door chime rang and Ken turned toward the door and said, "Come in."

The door slid open revealing a dour looking man in a grey suit carrying a black briefcase. His green eyes scanned the length of Ken and he said, "Lieutenant Pryce, may I come in?"

"Of course."

The man stepped in and offered his hand, "Dr. Kreig from LifeScapes. I understand you're checking out shortly and I just need to clear you for duty. It won't take long."

"Yes, I'm familiar with the process." Ken directed the doctor to a chair and he took a seat on the small sofa.

Dr. Kreig withdrew a small data pad from his pocket and tapped the surface to display Ken's client profile. "First, can you tell me your full name, date of birth, and current assignment?"

"Sure. Kendrick Miles Pryce, date of birth May fourth, 2266. My current assignment is Section Chief, Reclamation Engineering, aboard the SIS Pretoria."

"And your route?"

"We fly colony supply missions to Europa. Three years out, about nine months on station, then a little more than three years back."

"That's a helluva mission profile. I bet you really look forward to your layovers."

Ken stared into the man's eyes trying to betray no emotion. He shrugged, "Sure. It's nice to take a break, you know."

"Break? By the looks of your storyline you took a pretty long break." He shook his head as he read a summary of Ken's storyline from the data pad. "Almost *fifty* years of simulation time. It's impressive that you can wall it off so well."

Ken took a deep breath. "You get used to it."

"I was intrigued by your simulation. So many of our clients seem to prefer storylines with lots of action. You know, knights and castles and all that. Or, you know, the other ones where they're fabulously wealthy living lives of luxury on some island. Your's on the other hand, is quite unique. I'm sure our story architects enjoyed building something with so much, shall we say, *texture*."

After a long pause, Ken replied dryly, "I prefer the

simpler things."

Sensing the man's discomfort, Dr. Kreig decided to wrap up the visit quickly.

"Of course. So…any lingering issues I need to know about?"

"I'm feeling great, Doctor. A little tired, but I'm sure I just need a good night's sleep."

"Then I guess I can clear you for duty and get out of your hair. You probably have big plans for the rest of your layover."

Ken offered no further information.

Doctor Krieg lifted the briefcase and set it on his lap, opened it and said, "Before I go, I wanted to give you this. You selected the premium package." He lifted a brown leather photo album from the case and presented it to Ken with a bit too much ceremony.

The buttery softness of the cover triggered a flood of memories that almost overwhelmed Ken's senses. He lifted the book to his face and breathed deeply, savoring the earthy scent of the artificially aged leather. He opened the cover and saw the photograph that Will had taken on the beach the day before Maddie left for Mars. The three of them silhouetted against the setting sun.

"That's a nice memento." The doctor's face held the smile of a proud salesman.

Ken closed the cover and said quietly, "Thank you."

Both men stood and once again shook hands. They crossed the room to the door and the doctor turned and said, "Thank you for your service, Lieutenant. I know the life is, well…it has it's sacrifices. All of us at LifeScapes really admire the work you do out there. And we truly appreciate your business."

"Thank you, Doctor." Ken gave the man a thin smile.

An hour later Ken stood at the door of his stateroom aboard the Pretoria, the photo album tucked under his arm.

Another officer came around the corner and said, "Hey, Ken. I'm heading over to the club, you want to join me for some dinner and a few drinks?"

Ken turned to his comrade and offered a weak grin. "Thanks, but I'm going to hit the rack for a bit. Maybe tomorrow."

The officer nodded and smiled as he passed, replying, "Sure. But don't sleep away your whole layover."

Ken chuckled to himself at the unintentional irony. He touched his hand to the identification pad on the door and stepped into his dimly lit quarters. Standing inside the door, he looked around the small sitting room, noting the general clutter and trying to reclaim a feeling of familiarity. Crossing the room to the bookcase he took the photo album in his hands and slid it in place next to four other similar albums.

He threw himself into the single chair in the room, covered his face with his hands, and wept bitterly.

AUTHOR'S NOTE

The concept for this story was strongly influenced by my favorite Star Trek: The Next Generation episode, "The Inner Light." The brilliant original story was written by Morgan Gendel and the teleplay was penned by Morgan Gendel and Peter Allen Fields. It is one of the most beautiful and human stories in the Star Trek canon.

While preparing for another book series that tackles the technical, political, and human challenges posed by mankind's expansion into the solar system, I began thinking about some of the unique and new lifestyles that will emerge as humanity begins to make a permanent home in space. Entire new career fields will be created that will stretch the limits of the human mind, body, and psyche. Like our pioneer ancestors, the people who take the first tentative steps into the void will be people of extraordinary intelligence, determination, and commitment. They will be asked to make sacrifices that few people will be willing or able to make.

It is against this backdrop that I project the setting for my story. I was imagining what it would be like to be a regular worker, doing a mundane job on a spaceship that plies the vast interplanetary voids as it conducts the routine commerce of the next frontier. What would it be like to live on a spaceship for years, the entire time in microgravity, with little else but your work and the other crew members to provide the fullness of life? How would someone who chooses such a career conduct anything we would recognize as a normal life? How could they ever have a family? What would it be like to never be able to live on Earth again because your body has adapted to microgravity? And what kinds of unique solutions would we devise to compensate for the gigantic sacrifices such a vocation would naturally demand?

All of these questions drove me to take the kernel of a concept from the Star Trek episode and use it to construct what I think is a plausible and certainly interesting answer. I hope you enjoyed the story and encourage you to write a review on Amazon and tell your friends.

LaMonte M. Fowler
May 11, 2017
Elgin, Illinois

ABOUT THE AUTHOR

I was born in Honolulu, Hawaii but raised in Syracuse, New York. *(Like moving from Earth to Neptune.)* After a very thorough Catholic school education, I spent my 20's in a variety of interesting jobs until I discovered my aptitude for technology and sales.

Today, I am a husband and father of four amazing humans aged 30 to 19 living in suburban Chicago. I enjoy photography, reading, cooking, travel, and of course, writing.

My writing heroes are Arthur C. Clarke, Roger Zelazny, Orson Scott Card, David Wingrove, and C.S. Lewis.

You can find out more about my books and my second career as an independent author at my website lamontcmfowler.com. You can subscribe to my mailing list on my website "contact" page. Follow me on Twitter.com @MontyFowler. And lastly, please visit and "Like" my Facebook page at www.facebook.com/lamontemfowler.

www.ingramcontent.com/pod-product-compliance
Lightning Source LLC
Chambersburg PA
CBHW070650130626
46555CB00006B/2805